OKRA STEW

A Gullah Geechee Family Celebration

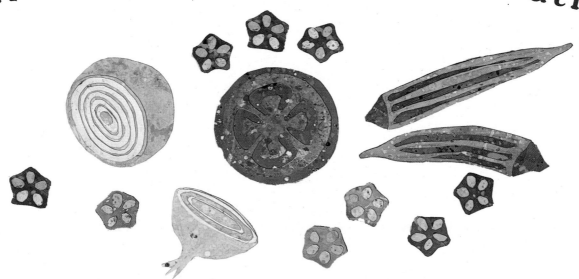

Henry Holt and Company, *Publishers since 1866*
Henry Holt® is a registered trademark of Macmillan Publishing Group, LLC
120 Broadway, New York, NY 10271 • mackids.com

Our books may be purchased in bulk for promotional, educational, or business use.
Please contact your local bookseller or the Macmillan Corporate and Premium Sales Department at
(800) 221-7945 ext. 5442 or by email at MacmillanSpecialMarkets@macmillan.com.

Library of Congress Cataloging-in-Publication Data is available.

First edition, 2023
Book design by Asher Caswell
Printed in China by Hung Hing Off-set Printing Co. Ltd.,
Heshan City, Guangdong Province

ISBN 978-1-250-84966-3 (hardcover)

1   3   5   7   9   10   8   6   4   2

The art for this book was created with acrylic paint,
hand-painted paper, textiles, and natural materials.

I dedicate this book to Ron, Sara, and
Simeon; Shannon for holding my hand;
my daddy who taught me to garden;
and the ancestors for their example.

OKRA STEW
A Gullah Geechee Family Celebration

By Natalie Daise

Henry Holt and Company

New York

Cardinal bird sings me awake in the early dark.
"Dayclean soon!
Dayclean soon!"

I sing back, **"Good morning to you, how oona fa do?"** and hop out of bed to see what Papa and I are doing today.

In the kitchen, Papa puts a warm biscuit on my plate with butter and honey.

I take a bite.

The biscuit is soft, the butter is salty,
and the honey is sticky and sweet.
Mmmm!

"What are you two up to this morning?" asks Mama.
"Oh, Bobo and I have lots to do. Tonight we're cooking okra stew," Papa replies.

"That sounds good, son!" Grandpa says.

"Oooh," says Big Sis with a grin, "I can't wait!"

"Have fun," Mama says.
She hugs me goodbye before she leaves
for work and takes Big Sis to school.
I grab another biscuit. Mmmm.
I can't wait either!

Dayclean comes with the rising sun. The garden air smells fresh and green. Morning glories grow purple over the fence.

The crepe myrtle blossoms are humming with bees. **"Busy picking pollen, busy picking pollen,"** they buzz.

I sing back, **"Me and my papa, out in the garden, picking some veggies for okra stew!"**

Papa smiles. He picks the rough green pods from the tall okra plants and tosses them in the basket. I snap smooth red tomatoes from the vines and plop them in too.

With our basket full we go back to the house. Grandpa sits
on the porch sewing baskets, his hands moving quickly.
The pile of grass beside his chair smells warm and sweet.

"What you got there?"
he asks as he looks in my basket.
"Well, look at you!"

I crouch down low to see what's here —
seashells and seagulls, fiddler crabs and turtles.
They scurry across the wet sand.

"Run, run, fiddle crab, run and hide.
Coota got a shell to hide inside!" I sing.

Soon my bucket is full of shells and
Papa's bucket is full of shrimp.
"Well, Bobo," he says.
"Do you think that's enough?"
"Yes!" I shout.

In the kitchen, I stand on my stool and
wash the okra and tomatoes in the sink.
Papa cuts them with his knife.

Chop
chop the okra.

Slice
slice
the tomatoes.

In go the seasonings — salt and pepper, garlic and herbs.
"Is this how your daddy used to make it?" I ask.

Papa nods. **"Mm-hmm. He taught me how right here in this kitchen."**
I take in a deep breath of the spicy scent.
When the stew begins to bubble and pop, we add in the shrimp.
Plop. Plop.

"Let's make some cornbread," Papa says.
He takes Nana's big green bowl from the cupboard.
It's the bowl she used when Papa was a little boy.

I pour cornmeal
into it.

Papa grabs the eggs.

Crack
crack!

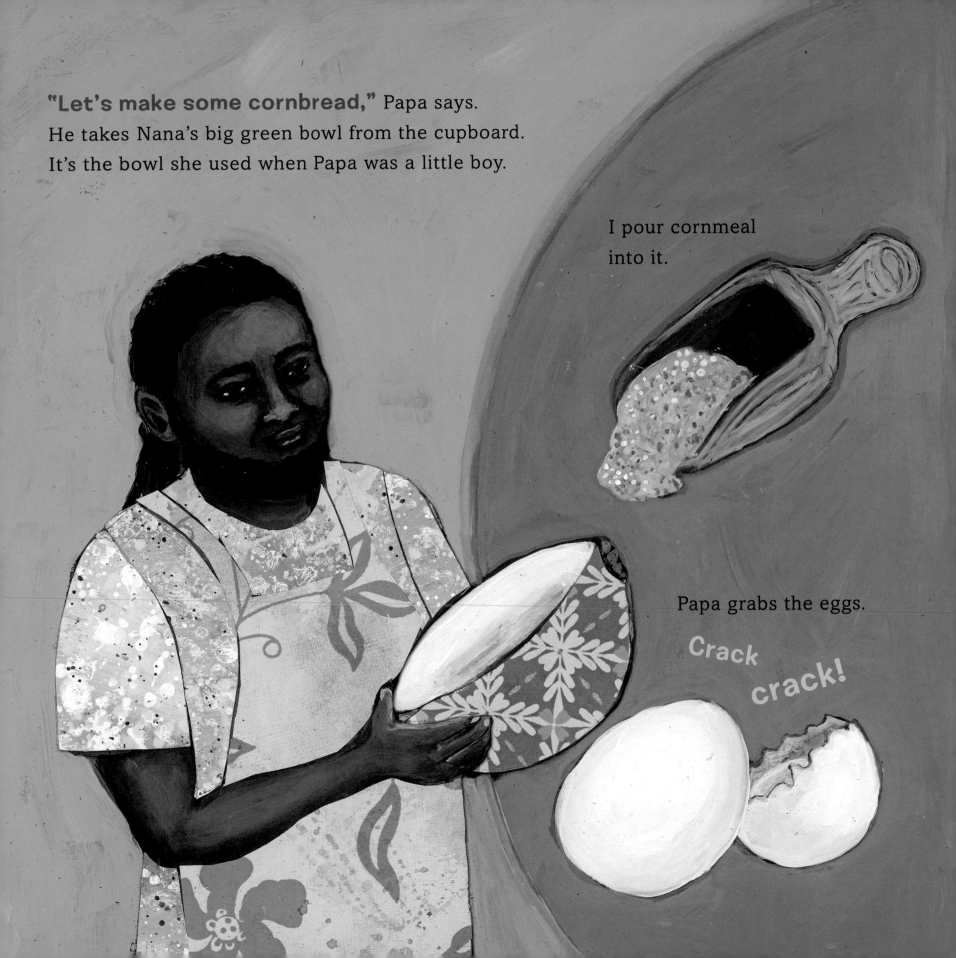

Papa turns the cornbread batter into the old black skillet that Great-Grandma used for fried fish and chicken and long-ago meals. He puts it in the oven. It will be ready soon!

Papa laughs and sings, **"Dat's fa true, gotta have rice with okra stew!"** I know rice goes with almost everything. The rice rains down into the pot. I shake in some salt and put on the top.

When the sun red fa down,
Mama comes home.

"Hey there, little one!"
she says with a hug.
"What did you do today?"
Papa and I grin.

There's rice in the rice pot, stew in the stewpot, cornbread in the skillet. The scents all swirl in the air.

Big Sis sniffs. "Mmm. It smells good in here!"

"Sure does," says Grandpa.

The cornbread is sweet like memory,
the rest of the meal is too.
My family and I hold hands 'round the table.
I sing, **"Tenky for Grandpa, Mama,
and Sis too. Tenky for Papa
and okra stew!"**

A NOTE FROM THE AUTHOR
on Gullah Geechee Culture and History

Origins of the Gullah Geechee People

Okra Stew is set in the Gullah Geechee community, which extends in the United States from Wilmington, North Carolina, down the Atlantic coast to Saint Augustine, Florida. The Gullah Geechee people are descendants of the West Africans who were enslaved from rice-producing countries—among them Senegal, Gambia, Guinea, Guinea-Bissau, Sierra Leone, and Liberia—and brought to the American coastal Lowcountry to produce cash crops, the most prolific of which was rice. They brought with them their skills and knowledge of agriculture and rice production, spiritual beliefs, and dietary practices. Even today, rice, seafood, and garden-fresh stews are an integral part of the cultural diet.

Gullah Geechee Cultural Practices in the Book

The words and images in *Okra Stew* bear witness to many Gullah Geechee cultural practices. Honoring the elders and ancestors is an important part of the culture. This is evident by the okra stew recipe and the cooking utensils, which have been passed down through generations. Protecting the home by placing blue bottles on trees and painting the trim around doors and windows blue is also a cultural practice. And leaving a broom by the door keeps those with ill intent from entering. It is common to have multigenerational homes, where the children can be cared for by the elders. The making of sweetgrass baskets is a hallmark of the culture. These coil baskets are sewn together with marsh grass, pine straw, and palm leaf, and are still made today as they were made in West Africa generations ago, carried across the ocean in the memory of the ancestors.

Gullah Language

The Creole language, known as Gullah, also arrived with the West African ancestors and is still spoken in our community. A few Gullah words and phrases are used in *Okra Stew*:

Dayclean: morning

Oona: you (singular or plural).
Example: "How oona fa do?": "How are you doing?"

Fiddle crab: a variation of fiddler crab,
a small sand and marsh crab found in the Lowcountry

Coota: turtle

Dat's fa true: that's true

When the sun red fa down: at sunset

A Personal Connection to the Story

In many ways, this book is deeply personal. Bobo is not only the child's name—it was once a traditional Gullah name given to a boy child born on a Monday, as was my own son. His father has always called him Bobo. My father planted the gardens in our backyard when I was a child, and I am honored to own the cast-iron pans of my great-grandmother and the bowls that were passed down from my husband's mother. The garden in the book reflects my own—the morning glories over the fence, the bees in the crepe myrtle, the blue bottles, and the cardinals singing the sun up.

The Spirit of Sankofa

Okra Stew is written and illustrated in the spirit of *sankofa*, a word from the Twi language of Ghana, which means "go back and fetch it," or to reach back to the past for that which is good and bring it with us into the future. This is one of the adinkra symbols that represent this principal, and I use it often in my work.

MY OKRA STEW RECIPE

I never saw my great-grandmother use a recipe. And while I have used recipes for all kinds of things, stews are often composed by feel and whatever is at hand. But I know how important it is to pass traditions from one generation to the next, so I'll do my best to detail my process.

Serving size: four portions

Ingredients:

- 2 tbsp. olive oil
- 1 large onion, chopped
- 2 or 3 cloves garlic, minced
- 1 green pepper, chopped
  Or whatever pepper you pulled from your garden or bought at your local store— you might like a little more heat. I do.
- 2 or 3 fresh tomatoes, chopped
- 1 28-oz. can diced tomatoes
- 32 oz. chicken or vegetable broth
- 1 bay leaf
- Salt
- ½ pound okra, chopped (about 2 cups) *Frozen chopped okra can be used if you don't have fresh.*
- Miscellaneous veggies: frozen or canned lima beans and fresh-cut, frozen, or canned corn
- Black pepper
- Red pepper flakes
- 1 pound shrimp, peeled and deveined
- Optional: fresh herbs
  I like to use marjoram from my garden.
- Rice, cooked

1. Heat olive oil in a large stewpot or Dutch oven over medium-low to medium heat.
2. Add the onion and stir until softened.
3. Add the garlic and green pepper. Cook for a few more minutes until garlic softens.
4. Add fresh tomatoes, canned tomatoes, broth, bay leaf, fresh herbs (if using), and 1 to 2 tsp of salt. Bring to a low simmer.
5. When broth reaches a simmer, add the okra, other veggies (drain first, if canned), as well as black pepper and a generous shake of red pepper flakes.
6. Bring back to a simmer and stir occasionally until broth begins to thicken, about 20 minutes.
7. Toss in the peeled and deveined shrimp and allow shrimp to cook until it becomes pink, about 5 or 6 more minutes.
8. Add more salt and pepper to taste.
9. Remove bay leaf and serve over rice!

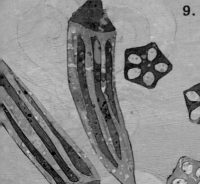
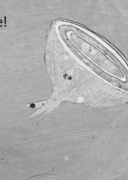